Printed in the U.S.A.

ISBN 0-7172-8333-X

JIM HENSON'S MUPPETS IN

I'm Sorry!

A Book About Apologizing

By Daphne Skinner • Illustrated by Joel Schick

GROLIER

It was a foggy Sunday afternoon—a perfect day for the movies. Kermit stood outside the theater waiting eagerly for Fozzie. He was really looking forward to seeing *Revenge of the Killer Flies* with his best friend. The poster for it looked very scary and exciting.

Kermit checked his watch. Yikes! It was getting late. Where was Fozzie?

Meanwhile, Fozzie was checking his watch, too. But he was not on his way to *Revenge of the Killer Flies*. No—Fozzie was standing in front of a different movie theater several blocks away. He was waiting to see *Return of the Mutant Bees*.

The movie was starting. But where was Kermit? Fozzie watched anxiously as everyone rushed into the theater. He was missing the beginning of the movie! Plus, the fog had changed to rain—pouring rain. Fozzie stood there for as long as he could. Finally, wet and disappointed, he went into the theater.

Three hours later, Fozzie and Kermit were talking on the phone, and they were having a fight—a big fight.

"What do you mean, it was my fault?" Kermit said. "I *told* you to meet me at *Revenge of the Killer Flies*. You got the name of the movie wrong. Why don't you admit it and say you're sorry?"

"I will not!" Fozzie said. "You told me the wrong movie and now *you* won't admit it. I missed the first fifteen minutes, which everyone says is the best part. And I got all wet waiting for you. You're the one who should apologize." Fozzie was so angry that he slammed down the phone.

The next morning, Kermit and Fozzie were still angry. They didn't sit next to each other on the school bus the way they always did.

They avoided each other in class.

They didn't share their lunches.

They didn't talk. They didn't even look at one another.

It's Kermit's fault, thought Fozzie.

It's Fozzie's fault, thought Kermit.

In geography class that afternoon, Mr. Bumper said he wanted everyone to learn how to make maps. "We'll start by drawing a map of the United States," he said. "Your maps will be due on Friday. To make things easier and more fun, let's work in teams," he added.

Mr. Bumper picked several teams, and then he looked at Kermit and Fozzie. "Why don't you two work together?" he said.

Kermit didn't know what to say. How could he and Fozzie work together when they weren't even talking?

Fozzie didn't know what to say, either. He felt angry and sad and mixed up, all at the same time. He hated fighting with Kermit, and he wanted everything to be normal again. But why should he have to apologize when it was all Kermit's fault?

Everyone in the classroom busily began making plans to work together. Everyone, that is, but Fozzie and Kermit. How could they make plans? They couldn't even figure out how to stop fighting.

When the bell rang, Piggy came up to Kermit and Fozzie. "Skeeter and I are going to start on our map this afternoon," said Piggy. "How about you two?"

"I guess we'll be starting this afternoon," said Kermit glumly. "Unless Fozzie has some kind of problem with that."

"Tell Kermit," Fozzie said to Piggy, "that *my* only problem is with people who don't show up when they're supposed to."

"You can tell Fozzie," Kermit said to Piggy, "that I will be at his house at four o'clock. And he'd better be there and not somewhere else!"

When Kermit rang Fozzie's bell at four
o'clock, Fozzie's dad opened the door. He was
carrying Baby Freddie, Fozzie's little brother.

"Come on in, Kermit," he said. "Fozzie's
working at the kitchen table. And Fred and I
are baking a cake."

Kermit could tell Fozzie's dad knew about
the fight. He looked just a little worried.

Kermit walked slowly into the kitchen. Fozzie barely looked up when he came in. All he did was push a note over to Kermit.

"I'll draw the states. You color them in. Okay?" it said.

Kermit picked up a crayon. "Okay," he wrote. But he sure didn't feel okay. Fighting was no fun at all.

Suddenly, there was a loud *splat!* and then a squishy *thunk!*

Fozzie's dad whirled around. Freddie had poured the banana frosting onto the counter and then slapped a wooden spoon on top of it.

"Freddie!" groaned Fozzie's dad. "I told you not to play with the frosting! Look at you! You're a mess!" He scooped Freddie up. "You're going into the bathtub right now."

Freddie began to sniffle as he was carried out of the room.

"Sorry, Daddy," he said in a tiny voice. "Sorry."

Freddie's words hung in the air long after he was gone. Kermit and Fozzie looked at each other. In that moment, they both knew what to say to end their terrible fight.

"Fozzie!" said Kermit. "I'm sorry."

"I'm sorry, too," said Fozzie. "Really."

"I shouldn't have said you were wrong," said Kermit.

"And I shouldn't have blamed everything on you," said Fozzie. "Besides, maybe I did make a mistake."

"It doesn't matter," said Kermit. "Let's just be friends again, okay?"

"Deal!" said Fozzie. The two friends smiled at each other. Everything was all right again. What a relief!

Half an hour later, Fozzie's dad came back into the kitchen carrying Freddie.

"We're finished, Dad," Fozzie told him. "What do you think of our map?" Every state was there, neatly colored in and labeled.

"You made a great map, boys!" said Fozzie's dad.

"And we made friends, too," said Fozzie.

"It's not easy to say you're sorry," said Fozzie's dad. "But it's really worth it. Isn't it, Freddie?" He gave the baby a hug.

Freddie saw the cake on the counter. "Cake!" he said.

"Great idea!" said Fozzie's dad. "Cake for a celebration."

And on that, Fozzie and Kermit couldn't disagree.

Let's Talk About Apologizing

Admitting that you were wrong can be one of the hardest things in the world to do. It certainly was for Fozzie and Kermit. But it was a good thing they said those two little words—*I'm sorry*. Otherwise, who knows when they would have started talking again?

Here are some questions about apologizing for you to think about:

Did you ever tell someone you were sorry? Was it hard?

Why do you think it's sometimes difficult to apologize?

Did someone ever apologize to you? What happened? How did you feel?